W9-AHA-698

→ SPECIAL EDITION ←

SPIROS
THE GHOST PHOENIX

ADAM BLADE
ILLUSTRATED BY EZRA TUCKER

SCHOLASTIC INC.
New York Toronto London Auckland Sydney
Mexico City New Delhi Hong Kong Buenos Aires

With special thanks to Michael Ford

To three young heroes — Charlie, Alex, and Tom

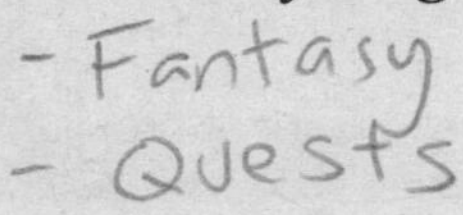

ISBN-13: 978-0-545-13267-1
ISBN-10: 0-545-13267-3

Beast Quest series created by Working Partners Ltd., London.

Published by Scholastic Inc., 557 Broadway, New York, NY 10012, by arrangement with Working Partners Ltd.

12 11 10 9 8 7 6 5 4 3 9/10 11 12 13 14/0

Designed by Tim Hall
Printed in the U.S.A.
First printing, July 2009

Special Edition

Heroes and Villains

Tom

PREFERRED WEAPON: Sword
ALSO CARRIES: Magical Shield, Destiny Compass
SPECIAL SKILLS: Tom's uncle is a blacksmith, so he knows all about metals and material strength. Plus, every journey gains him new abilities, so he also has incredible vision, speed, strength, and bravery.

Elenna

PREFERRED WEAPON: Bow & Arrow

ALSO CARRIES: Nothing. Between her bow and her wolf, Silver, Elenna doesn't need anything else!

SPECIAL SKILLS: Not only is Elenna an expert hunter, she is also knowledgeable about boats and water. But most importantly, she can think quickly in tight spots, which has helped Tom more than once!

Storm

Tom's horse, a gift from King Hugo. Storm's good instincts and speed have helped Tom and Elenna from the very beginning.

Silver

Elenna's tame wolf and constant companion. Not only is Silver good to have on their side in a fight, but the wolf can also help Tom and Elenna find food when they're hungry.

Aduro

The good wizard of Avantia and one of Tom's closest allies. Aduro has helped Tom many times, but when Aduro was captured by Malvel, Tom was able to help the good wizard by rescuing him.

Malvel

Tom's enemy, determined to enslave the Beasts of Avantia and defeat Tom. This evil wizard rarely shows himself, but if he does, Tom can be sure that danger is near.

THE BEASTS OF AVANTIA

FERNO

THE FIRE
DRAGON

SEPRON

THE SEA
SERPENT

CYPHER

THE MOUNTAIN
GIANT

Tagus
The Night Horse

Tartok
The Ice Beast

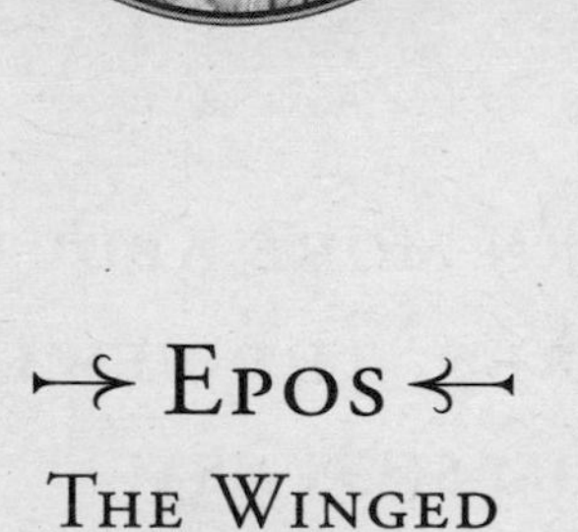

Epos
The Winged Flame

→ SPIROS ←

THE GHOST PHOENIX

→ NAWDREN ←

THE BLACK PHOENIX

READ ON TO LEARN MORE ABOUT SPIROS AND NAWDREN, THE NEWEST BEASTS IN TOM'S QUEST!

Story One

Chapter One

The Evil of Malvel

"Do you realize where we are, Tom?" said Elenna, as he helped her over a fallen trunk. Silver bounded over to stand beside Tom's stallion, Storm.

Tom peered through the dense trees. It had been raining, and the smell of damp leaves filled his nostrils. "In a forest?" he joked.

"This is where we first met!" said Elenna.

Tom thought back. He'd been on a mission to free Ferno the Fire Dragon from Wizard Malvel's evil curse. "It was my first Beast Quest," he said. "You were hunting rabbits with Silver."

"That's right," said Elenna, stroking Silver's neck. "The forest doesn't seem as frightening now."

Tom nodded. After all the Beasts they'd faced together, the darkness of the forest no longer made him shiver. He placed his foot in Storm's stirrup and heaved himself up. Elenna climbed into the saddle behind him.

"Once we clear the forest and cross the plains, it's only a short ride to Errinel," said Elenna.

Tom smiled. "I can't wait. It has been so long since I've seen my aunt and uncle. Something to eat and a soft bed is just what we need after all our adventures."

Silver barked and jumped up on his hind legs.

"And there might even be some bones for you!" Elenna laughed.

Tom steered his stallion across the mossy forest floor. But something was bothering him. He sensed

that he and his friends were not alone. He let his hand drop onto the hilt of his sword.

"What's wrong?" Elenna asked.

A sound like a crack of lightning splintered the silence, and a cloud of smoke appeared between the trees. Tom slipped from the saddle, unsheathing his sword and gripping his shield. Silver whimpered and Storm swished his tail.

"Is it Malvel?" whispered Elenna, dismounting.

But as the smoke cleared, a familiar figure emerged. He was wearing a cloak of faded blue-and-red silk.

"Aduro!" said Elenna, rushing forward.

Tom put away his sword. But the look in the old man's gray eyes made Tom anxious. "What is it, Aduro?" he asked.

"I had to come immediately," said the good wizard.

Even Silver had stopped leaping now, and Elenna fell back beside Tom.

Aduro stroked his wispy beard. "Tom, Elenna, you must steel yourselves for terrible news," he warned. "Malvel has committed his worst crime yet."

Fear crept over Tom's heart. He felt Elenna's fingers grip his arm.

Aduro looked Tom in the eye. "A messenger arrived at King Hugo's castle this morning with a dreadful tale. Last night, a weary traveler came to your village. The tavern owner thought there was something unusual about him, but your uncle Henry and aunt Maria, kind people that they are, gave him a meal and a bed for the night. This morning they were gone. And so was the traveler."

"Perhaps they offered to accompany him to his destination," said Tom.

"I'm afraid not," said Aduro. "The traveler left behind a message. . . ." The wizard pulled out a piece of parchment from his cloak and handed it to Tom.

He unfolded the thin paper and read: *"Dear Tom, your foolish quest will now hurt those closest to you. Malvel."*

"Oh, Tom!" gasped Elenna.

Tom felt sick. His hand clenched into a fist around the parchment. "I'll rescue Uncle Henry and Aunt Maria," he vowed. "I won't rest until I get them back."

Chapter Two

A New Beast

Tom looked at the good wizard. "Where are they now?" he asked.

Aduro shook his head sadly. "I've tried everything in my power, but I can't see where Malvel has taken them."

Tom felt anger flood through him. "How dare he? The fight is between Malvel and me. There was no reason to involve my family."

"Malvel's heart is dark," said Aduro. "He will hurt you any way he can."

Suddenly, a breeze blew through the clearing,

rustling the leaves. With it came the sound of a low cackle. Storm reared in fright.

"Malvel!" said Elenna.

Tom nodded. He'd recognize the laugh anywhere. "There must be some way to find out where they are," he said.

"What about the enchanted map?" said Elenna.

Tom dashed over to Storm and unlaced his saddlebag. The magical map of Avantia had helped them locate all the Beasts on their previous Quests. Perhaps it would help him find his aunt and uncle, too.

He knelt on the forest floor and unrolled the parchment. Elenna and Aduro stood over him. But no pulsing green line appeared to show him the way.

"Malvel's dark magic is strong." Aduro sighed. "He has overcome the power of the map."

"But there must be something we can do!" said Elenna.

"There may be one thing . . . ," the good wizard muttered. "No, no, it's too dangerous."

"What?" said Tom. "I'll do anything!"

Aduro placed both hands on Tom's shoulders. "If you want to rescue your aunt and uncle, you will have to undertake your toughest Quest yet. You must face another Beast, the likes of which you have never seen."

"I didn't know there were any others," said Tom.

"I'm talking of a Beast not seen for generations. The lost seventh Beast of Avantia."

Elenna gasped. "A seventh Beast?"

"Yes," said Aduro. "As well as the six good Beasts that patrol Avantia, there was a seventh created to guard the skies. She was born after the others. Let me show you."

The wizard brought his hands together in a loud clap that echoed through the forest, then he rubbed his palms. Tom looked on, baffled, and even Storm and Silver stepped closer. A thin trail of smoke emerged from between Aduro's clasped hands. It rose into the air, forming a cloud. Then, in the middle of the cloud, a shape emerged. It looked like a bird, but its wings were ablaze with a golden flame.

"Is that the seventh Beast?" asked Elenna.

"It is," said Aduro. "Her name is Spiros the Phoenix. If anyone can help you find where Malvel has taken Tom's aunt and uncle, it is Spiros. She is blessed with the power of All-Sight — magic that even I do not possess. It allows her to see into the far reaches of Avantia and beyond. Nothing is hidden from her."

The cloud of smoke evaporated into the forest, and with it the image of the phoenix.

"Where can we find her?" asked Tom.

Aduro frowned. "I wish it were that easy," he said. "But Spiros hasn't been seen in the skies of

Avantia for many years. No one knows where she is."

"How can that be?" asked Elenna.

"It was Malvel," said Aduro, his face darkening. "Before he bewitched the first six good Beasts, he also cast a spell over Spiros."

"What did he do to her?" asked Tom.

"He separated her body from her spirit," said the wizard.

Tom was confused. "How is that possible?" he asked. "Isn't she dead?"

"Not quite dead," said Aduro. "But halfway there. Spiros is a ghost!"

Elenna drew a sharp breath. A ghost phoenix!

"If you challenge Malvel again," said Aduro, "you will need all your bravery and wits to survive. It will be your most dangerous Quest yet."

But Tom had already made his decision. His aunt and uncle were his only family. He had to go.

He looked at Elenna. She was pale but gave a defiant nod. It was settled, then.

"We're ready," said Tom.

Aduro smiled. "I knew your courage would not fail. Now I must leave."

There was a flash near Aduro's feet that made Tom and Elenna step back. A curtain of smoke rose up, concealing him. When it disappeared, Aduro no longer stood before them.

"He's gone!" said Elenna.

"Come on," Tom said. "We need to track down Spiros. Let's get out of the forest." He led Elenna quickly through the trees, with Silver and Storm right behind them.

"But how are we going to find her?" asked Elenna. "She could be anywhere in Avantia. It might take years!"

Elenna was right. Even riding Storm at full

gallop, there was no telling how long their search would take.

Tom took out the map again. It showed the whole kingdom, as far as the icy plains in the north. "There must be a way!" he said. Then his eyes rested on the mountain where Ferno the Fire Dragon lived. It gave him an idea. "Wait, what if we used . . ."

". . . the good Beasts!" Elenna finished.

"Yes!" said Tom. "Avantia's too big for us to search quickly on our own, but with the help of the Beasts, it might be possible."

"Which one should we call first?" asked Elenna.

Tom pondered for a moment. "Ferno's mountain is close by. If this ghost phoenix patrols the skies, Ferno can help us search there. Perhaps the other Beasts will be able to help, too."

Tom rubbed the dragon's scale in his shield. But nothing stirred in the silence of the forest.

"Try again," said Elenna. "The Beasts won't let you down."

Tom did as she said, but not even a bird rustled in the branches.

Just as he was about to give up, a screech filled their ears, and ashes fluttered down around their feet. A shadow drifted above the trees.

"It's Ferno!" said Tom.

Chapter Three

The Good Dragon

FERNO CIRCLED ABOVE THE TREES, HIS JAGGED black wings blotting out the sun. Tom remembered how terrified he had been the first time he had seen the colossal creature's bloodred eyes, but now he was filled with pride.

Ferno opened his scaly wings to slow his descent. He landed gracefully in the clearing and strode toward them, his claws flattening the grass and his thick tail dragging across the ground. He towered above them, as tall as ten houses.

"Thank you for helping us!" shouted Tom.

Ferno lifted his head and blew out a stream of fire, filling the air with the bitter smell of sulfur. Storm whinnied a greeting.

The Beast folded his legs and lay on his stomach, leaving one wing extended toward them.

"He wants us to climb up," Tom said to Elenna.

"What about Storm and Silver?" she asked.

"There's room for them as well," said Tom as he scrambled up Ferno's wing. The scales felt hard and slippery beneath his hands. Elenna led Storm and Silver, and soon they were settled in the hollow between the dragon's shoulders. Ferno rose to his feet and opened his huge wings.

"Hold on tight!" Tom said.

Ferno charged through the clearing. The trees on the far side approached quickly, but the Beast showed no signs of slowing. Just when it seemed they would smash into the trees, Ferno launched

himself into the air. Tom whooped as the treetops fell away below them. The day was beautifully clear and he could see for miles. To the south, King Hugo's palace stood over the great city. Beyond that was Tom's home village of Errinel. Avantia looked so beautiful beneath them. It was difficult to think that Malvel's evil was once again at work.

"We need to find Spiros!" shouted Tom to Ferno. "We must search the skies."

The fire dragon seemed to understand, flying up beyond the clouds and circling in wide arcs. They searched until the sun reached its highest point, then they headed north. The temperature began to dip. Tom scanned the sky for any sign of the ghost phoenix, but he could see nothing apart from the occasional eagle.

Soon Ferno's wings were beating with less energy.

"It's too cold," said Elenna. "And Ferno's tired."

Tom patted the fire dragon's neck. "You've done enough, friend."

Ferno snorted and wheeled in the air, taking them back toward the grassy plains. A herd of cattle was grazing on the long grass. They scattered, letting out startled moos, when the mighty dragon dropped out of the sky and came to a stop.

Tom, Elenna, Storm, and Silver climbed down from Ferno's back, while the great Beast stood patiently.

"Thanks, old friend," said Tom. "You can go back to your mountain now."

With a farewell roar, the fire dragon took to the skies again.

Watching him fly away, Tom felt deflated. The golden chain mail he had won in his last Quest was meant to give him strength of heart, but right now he didn't feel like it was working. How would he ever find his aunt and uncle?

"We have to widen our search if we're going to find Spiros," he said. "What about the plains?"

"But they're vast," said Elenna. "Storm is strong, but even he can't cover so much ground."

"I know a Beast who can!" said Tom, and rubbed the fragment of horseshoe embedded in his shield.

After a few moments, the cattle began to crowd together.

"Something's spooked them," said Elenna.

Beneath Tom's feet, the ground quaked. The cows suddenly split into two groups, and a path opened up between them. A shape appeared on the horizon.

"Tagus!" Tom shouted. The soft rumble of hooves became louder as the horse-man galloped toward them. With the body of a stallion but the torso of a giant, he stood three times as tall as Storm. Shaggy black hair grew in a tangled mess on his head. He slowed in front of Tom and Elenna, his chest heaving as he pawed the ground.

"Welcome, Tagus," said Tom. "We have to find Spiros the Ghost Phoenix. Can you help us?"

Tagus couldn't speak, but he seemed to understand, and lowered himself to his knees so that Tom and Elenna could climb onto his back.

"Storm and Silver can stay here," Tom said as they mounted. "We'll have to go alone."

Storm was grazing contentedly, and Silver was already darting off into the long grass. Tom's legs gripped the Beast's middle and they set off at a canter over the plains.

Soon they were galloping through the grass at incredible speed. The feeling of power beneath

Tom was immense. It was impossible to speak over the thunder of Tagus's hooves, but he felt Elenna's fingers digging into his sides.

Tom scoured the grasslands for signs of Spiros and was beginning to give up hope, when he heard a wailing sound from behind a hillock. Tagus slowed to a trot. Could it be the ghost phoenix?

"That way!" shouted Tom. Tagus set off up the incline. As they neared the top, a howl pierced Tom's ears, followed by a low growl. A flash of brown appeared to their right. But it wasn't Spiros.

"Hyenas!" cried Elenna, placing an arrow to her bow.

Another creature skulked to their left, lifting its nose to sniff the air. Tagus swiveled on his hooves as Tom counted ten hyenas fanning out around them. He knew they wouldn't normally attack a Beast the size of Tagus, but weighed down with two humans, he must have seemed an easier target.

One of the ugly creatures darted at Tagus's leg and received a kick that sent him sprawling. Another followed, but Elenna fired an arrow, and with a yelp the hyena limped away.

"Good work," said Tom, then turned to see a large hyena bounding toward them. It leaped through the air, mouth slavering. There was no time to draw his sword, so Tom smashed his shield into the hyena's head. The creature fell to the ground, then dragged himself away, followed by the rest of the pack.

"That was close," said Elenna.

"Let's get away from here and keep searching," said Tom.

He steered the centaur toward the highest part of the plains, a plateau scattered with giant rocks. When they arrived at the top, Tom slipped from the Beast's back and clambered up one of the largest boulders, staring out across the plains. His golden helmet, safely locked away in King Hugo's castle, had given him the power of enhanced vision, and he trained it on every corner of the plains, desperately looking for a sign of the ghost phoenix.

"Anything?" Elenna asked.

Tom shook his head. "Nothing. And I'm not even sure how I'll recognize Spiros if she's a ghost." Tagus stood waiting for further commands. Tom turned to him. "Thank you, but you should go back to protecting your cattle."

Rearing onto his hind legs, Tagus roared, then galloped away, leaving Tom and Elenna alone.

"What now?" asked Elenna.

Tom smiled. "I have one more idea," he said. "Perhaps to find a phoenix, we need to use a phoenix."

"You don't mean . . ." began Elenna.

"That's right," said Tom. "We need Epos!"

→ CHAPTER FOUR ←

SEARCHING THE KINGDOM

TOM TOOK HIS SHIELD AND RUBBED THE feather of the Beast embedded there.

Almost immediately, a screech cut through the air, and a glow appeared on the horizon.

"There she is!" cried Elenna.

The glow grew into the shape of a winged creature. Tom felt his heart fill with joy. Epos's dark red feathers glittered in the sunlight, and flames trailed from the tips of her wings. She landed beside them, her talons clattering on the rocks.

Tom placed his foot on Epos's wing and climbed

up, settling into the thick feathers at the base of her neck. Elenna sat behind him.

Epos took to the air, gliding low over the plains. Then she flapped her wings and climbed higher.

"Keep your eyes open for Spiros," Tom said to Elenna.

He searched the sky for a flash of golden flame, but there was nothing. Tom steered Epos east, toward the volcano that was her home, but there was no sign of the seventh Beast there, either.

"Spiros!" he cried out in desperation. "Where are you?"

With a heavy heart, he guided the winged flame back to the plains where Storm and Silver were waiting.

As they jumped down from Epos's back, Silver dashed forward and placed his paws on Elenna's chest, licking her face. Storm nuzzled Tom with his nose.

"It's good to see you, too, boy," he said.

Epos took to the skies again, circled once, then gave a caw of farewell. Tom and Elenna waved good-bye.

"I think we need to try the northern mountains next," Tom said.

"Won't it be too cold for a phoenix there?" said Elenna.

"Too cold for a living phoenix, perhaps," replied Tom. "But not a ghost phoenix."

Mounting Storm, they galloped across the plains toward the foothills of the mountains. The sun started to dip from the sky, and the snowcapped mountains towered above them. If Tom could get up there, among the highest peaks of Avantia, he would be able to see the entire kingdom.

They ascended the mountain path, climbing toward a pass between two enormous peaks. Tom took out the last of their supplies from Storm's saddlebag — two Ruby Guya fruits from the depths of the Dark Jungle. The juice dripped down his chin as he ate, and it was just the boost of energy he needed.

Soon the air cooled and the path became difficult as they skirted the edge of the slope. Silver placed his paws carefully among the loose rocks, but Storm kept stumbling. Finally, as they reached an overhanging section of cliff, Tom drew up the reins.

"We can't go any farther on horseback," he said. "It's too dangerous. Storm and Silver should shelter here. We need a guide."

"Cypher?" asked Elenna.

Tom nodded. He rubbed the giant's token in his shield.

Silver lifted his nose into the air.

"What is it, boy?" asked Elenna.

A low rumbling echoed around them. Storm whinnied and took a few jittery steps backward.

From a ridge opposite, a section of rocks crumbled and crashed down into the valley.

"Is it a landslide?" asked Elenna.

Before Tom could answer, a huge hairy hand appeared over the edge of a cliff ahead. The claws were yellow and as thick as wooden planks. Cypher the Mountain Giant heaved himself over the precipice.

Each of his legs was as thick as a tree trunk, and his muscular arms looked as if they could smash buildings to pieces. When Cypher saw them, he let out a roar, and his face split into a wide grin, revealing brown, crooked teeth. His single eye twinkled with kindness.

"Cypher, it's you, thank goodness!" Tom shouted. Then he pointed to the highest mountains. "We need to go up there. Can you take us?"

Cypher turned his massive head in the direction of the snowy peaks, then scooped Tom up with one hand. With the other he grabbed Elenna. She let out a little squeal, which turned into a laugh. The Beast was gentle, and the pads of his palms were as soft and warm as worn leather.

Leaving Storm and Silver beneath the overhang, Cypher carried Tom and Elenna higher into the peaks. Rocks scattered from his giant feet. At one point, a line of trees blocked their route, but Cypher pushed them aside, bending the trunks like twigs. As they passed through, the trees sprang upright again, showering the ground with leaves.

Soon they reached the snow. Tom peered over the top of the giant's warm fist to look out for signs of Spiros. They checked behind huge boulders and in shallow gorges. As the snow became deeper, Cypher's feet left indentations as long and wide as market carts. But there was no sign of other life in the snow.

The mountain giant set Tom and Elenna down carefully for a moment's rest. Tom immediately scanned the horizon with his magical sight. There was nothing to see but the lonely, jagged peaks.

Fresh flakes of snow had started to fall. Tom shivered. He wondered if the snowstorm was sent by Malvel to frustrate him. Tom had used four Beasts already, and he was no closer to finding Spiros. Malvel was winning. Tom let out a shout of frustration that echoed across the mountain range. Without Spiros and her gift of All-Sight, he would never be able to rescue his aunt and uncle from Malvel's clutches.

"I've failed," he muttered.

Then he felt Elenna's hand on his shoulder.

"This isn't over," she said. "We mustn't give up the search."

"Where else is there to look?" said Tom. "I've used almost all of the good Beasts, and we still can't find Spiros."

Elenna's face lit up.

"What is it?" Tom asked.

"I do have one idea," she replied. "Didn't Aduro tell us that Spiros was born after all the other six Beasts, to patrol the skies?"

"I think so, yes. Why is that important?"

"Don't you see?" said Elenna. "She was the seventh Beast to arrive. Perhaps if we get all six Beasts together, in one place . . ."

Tom stood up and gripped Elenna by the shoulders. "Spiros will return!" he said. "Yes! Of course. Six came before her, now six must come again!"

→ Chapter Five ←

Summoning the Ghost Phoenix

The sky had darkened. Looking to the west, Tom could see the sun was nearing the horizon. It was snowing heavily now, and the icy flakes tickled his face.

"It'll be night soon," he said. "We have to get back down to Storm and Silver."

Cypher scooped them up once more. Tom felt exhilarated as the Beast ran down the mountain in bounding strides. If their new plan worked, they'd find Spiros and save his aunt and uncle from Malvel.

Once they were near the foothills, they said good-bye to Cypher.

"We know the way from here," said Tom. "But we may need you again soon."

The mountain giant grunted, then trudged off through the snow. Tom and Elenna slid down the rest of the slope on their behinds, whooping with delight. Storm and Silver were waiting where they'd left them, sheltered under the rocks.

Tom took blankets from Storm's saddlebag. He gave one to Elenna and wrapped the other around his shoulders. Silver's thick coat would keep him warm. Then Tom led his three companions to the base of the mountains by the light of the moon, which glowed faintly behind thin shreds of mist.

"We need to get to the Western Ocean by dawn," he said. "We have to find Sepron, then summon the other Beasts there. I'm afraid we won't be able to rest tonight."

"I feel more awake than ever," said Elenna. "And so does Silver, by the look of him."

Her wolf was alert, with his ears pricked and his tail up.

Tom patted Storm's flank. "I think Storm will be able to keep going, too."

The stallion snorted, and bucked his hind legs.

With Tom and Elenna on his back, Storm charged into the night. Tom could hear Elenna's teeth chattering behind him, but she didn't complain. The stars flickered above as bats swooped around them.

It was a cold dawn when they reached the Western Ocean, but Tom's blood felt warm. The sea was calm, with only light ripples disturbing the surface.

Storm stopped on the pebbled shoreline, and Silver ran ahead to splash in the shallows. Tom knew what he had to do. He pulled his shield off his shoulder and threaded his hand into the strap. The serpent's tooth would draw Sepron to him.

Tom rubbed his sleeve against the tooth, then held the shield's face toward the sea.

A wave traveled along the water, crashing into the beach. Silver scurried away from the edge.

"There's something out there," said Elenna.

A larger wave, almost as high as Tom's waist, came in with the swell. Then a hundred paces offshore, something broke the surface — a flash of colors like a rainbow.

"It's Sepron!" whispered Tom. The multicolored scales appeared again, fifty paces out. The sea serpent was swimming toward them.

Sepron's head reared out of the shallows and rose up on a slender green neck. He opened his mouth to reveal curved fangs. Slimy seaweed was tangled in his gaping jaws. But Tom knew that behind the terrifying appearance, Sepron was a good Beast.

The serpent crashed into the water again, sending up a wall of spray that soaked Tom and Elenna. Tom couldn't help laughing, and Elenna burst into giggles.

"It's time to put our theory to the test," said Tom. Turning to face the mainland, he held out his shield, sending out his summons to the other five Beasts. "Good Beasts of Avantia. Unite!"

The wood began to shake on his arm. As the shield vibrated, Tom forced his arm to continue holding it out. All the magical symbols — the scale, the tooth, the tear, the horseshoe piece, the claw, and the feather — glowed in the dawn light. His shoulder screamed in pain, and he gritted his teeth. It was the most powerful sorcery Tom had ever experienced. *I have to go through with it,* he thought.

"Tom, look!" shouted Elenna. "The Beasts are coming!"

Tom lowered his shield. His heart almost stopped at the sight. Standing at the edge of the beach were the other five Beasts. Cypher stood beside Tagus, whose dark hair was wet with pearls of dew. Ferno stood at one end of the row and blew a spurt of fire, with Epos hovering at the other end of the row, her flaming feathers adding light to the gloomy morning. And finally, Tartok stepped forward, her shaggy fur grubby after traveling so far from the icy plains.

"They're all here!" said Tom happily.

Cypher plucked both Elenna and Tom from the ground, placing them on his shoulders, and Tom at once looked inland for any sign of Spiros. The mist was beginning to lift now, and as time passed, the sun's light grew stronger. What if he was wrong? What if Spiros couldn't be tempted to come to them?

"Now what?" said Elenna, but almost as soon as she had spoken the words, Ferno thumped the pebbles with his tail. Tartok roared and Cypher bellowed. Tagus reared on his horse's legs and stamped the ground. Ferno lifted her beak and gave a deafening screech. Finally, Sepron splashed in the water, sending up huge waves. Soon the cries of all six Beasts echoed across the dawn, making Tom's skin tingle.

"They're calling for Spiros," he shouted over the din.

A screech penetrated the mist. Tom turned on Cypher's shoulders. The Beasts twisted their mighty heads to look. Silver was barking excitedly, and Storm whinnied, pacing up and down on the shore.

"Look!" said Elenna, pointing.

Tom peered to a spot in the sky. It looked at first as though the stars were still out — a patch of the sky sparkled even though it was daytime.

Then a shape, no more than a shadow, appeared above the sea fog. It moved quickly, soaring toward them. Tom wasn't afraid. This is what he'd been waiting for. Spiros the Ghost Phoenix was coming!

→ CHAPTER SIX ←

JOURNEY ABOVE THE CLOUDS

SPIROS SOARED ACROSS THE SKY, WEAVING IN and out of the clouds. The feathers of her body were as red as polished rubies, but the wings were golden. Her eyes were emerald green, and she was surrounded by a luminous mist.

"She's beautiful!" gasped Elenna.

Tom tapped Cypher's shoulder, and the Beast lowered him and Elenna to the ground. Tom called up to Spiros. "I have to find where Malvel has taken my aunt and uncle!"

Spiros twisted her wings and came to hover in the air above.

"I think she wants us to go with her," said Tom.

"We can't ride a ghost phoenix!" Elenna said.

"But we can follow one!" said Tom.

"Of course!" said Elenna, and together they dashed toward Epos and climbed up onto her back. Storm trotted forward and lowered his head. Tom could tell his brave stallion was sad to be saying good-bye to his master again. Silver appeared at his side and gave a high-pitched whine.

"We'll be back soon!" said Tom. "But this part of the Quest is too dangerous for you two."

Ferno extended a giant wing over the two animals.

"He'll look after them," said Elenna. "Good-bye, Silver. Good-bye, Storm!"

Epos left the ground with a flap of her wings, and the other Beasts grew small as the flame bird broke through the layer of cloud into the clear blue sky. Spiros turned and flew north, her specter-like form gliding through the air like a wisp of colored mist.

Epos set off in pursuit.

"Where do you think she's taking us?" asked Elenna.

"I don't know," said Tom, pulling his silver compass from his pocket. The needle wavered, before pointing toward Destiny. But as they watched, it suddenly swung around — and signaled Danger.

"It can't be both," said Elenna. She gasped as the needle swung back to Destiny again.

"Perhaps it can," said Tom, putting the instrument away. "We have no choice. We have to trust Spiros and her gift of All-Sight."

They soared ahead, flying among the tallest of the mountain peaks that broke through the cloud. Despite the wind whistling past their ears and flattening their clothes against their bodies, everything was eerily calm. Spiros's golden wings, shifting in and out of focus, glinted in the sunlight.

"We must be traveling to the icy plains, to Tartok's land," Tom said.

"But nothing can live there," said Elenna. "It's too cold."

Tom knew she was right. If his aunt and uncle had been taken there, perhaps he was too late. But he couldn't give up hope. Aduro had told him that Spiros could help, and he wouldn't lose faith now.

They left the mountains behind. Although the sky ahead was clear, something didn't feel right.

"Elenna," he whispered, "I don't think we're alone."

"I know," she said with a shiver. "I feel it, too."

Suddenly, a shriek filled Tom's ears, and they

were cast in shadow. Tom and Elenna swiveled around. There was another phoenix! It was the same size and shape as Spiros, but its feathers were black and it smelled of rotting flesh. Instead of scattering radiant light, it rained sulfurous, hot ash. Its talons looked as if they were made of charred iron.

"It's disgusting!" said Elenna.

The black phoenix dipped a wing and swooped toward them.

"Hold on!" Tom shouted, and leaned forward, tugging at Epos's feathers. The flame bird rolled to one side, and the black phoenix's talons brushed past Tom's shoulder. Epos continued to roll, and for a moment, Tom felt completely weightless as the world turned upside down. Elenna cried out behind him, and her arms tightened around his middle. Then Epos turned full circle and righted herself.

Tom saw that the material of his tunic was torn at the top of his arm. Any closer, and the Beast's talons would have taken off his head.

But as the black phoenix climbed again, Tom saw something else. Riding on the evil creature's back was a girl with a pale face. Her long dark hair flowed in the wind and she stared at Tom with coal-black eyes.

"Who is *that*?" shouted Elenna.

Tom didn't have time to answer. The girl was already drawing her sword.

Chapter Seven

Duel in the Skies

The black phoenix closed in on them again, and Tom just had time to draw his own sword as the girl brought hers down. He parried the blow, but the force nearly knocked him off Epos's back.

The black phoenix climbed high above them, preparing for another attack. Spiros remained at a safe distance. Tom knew there was nothing she could do.

"That girl must be one of Malvel's agents!" said Elenna.

"Keep low," said Tom, raising his sword as the girl guided her phoenix toward them again.

"Attack!" she screamed.

As it swooped down, the black phoenix plunged its talons into Epos's side. The flame bird let out a pained cry as a clump of her feathers was torn away. Tom felt Elenna's hands loosen on his waist.

"Help!" she screamed. Tom twisted around to see that Elenna had slipped off the Beast's back and was clinging desperately to Epos's wing. Keeping a firm grip on Epos's neck feathers with one hand, Tom sheathed his sword and reached down with his free arm.

"Grab my hand!" he shouted.

Elenna's face was pale with fear, and her knuckles were white. "I can't let go," she yelled back. "I'll fall!"

Tom reached down, feeling the sinews in his arm stretch. Just a little farther and he'd be able to reach his friend. . . .

Then he heard a thud. Epos screeched. The girl's black phoenix was attacking again. Tom felt the flame bird tip to one side, and it was all he could do to hang on. Spiros was above them now, squawking desperately. Elenna lost her grip. Her fingers slipped through Epos's feathers and she cried out in terror as she plummeted through the sky. Then the sounds of her screams were lost as she disappeared into the mist.

"No!" yelled Tom. He took off his shield and threw it after her with all his might. "Elenna," he shouted. "Use my shield!" There was a chance that its magic would stop her falling — if she could catch it. Tom steered Epos

down into the clouds after Elenna, but the black phoenix blocked his path. The pale-faced girl let out a cackle.

"You'll pay for what you've done," Tom replied, his anger swelling.

"We'll see about that," said the girl. There was something familiar about her face — but Tom had no time to think where he might have seen her before. The girl was flying at him again.

This time Tom was ready. Their swords met with a clang that sent a shock wave down Tom's arm. He swung a blow at her, but she ducked out of the way, as quick as lightning. Epos locked talons with the black phoenix, her sharp beak darting at the evil creature's throat. The air was filled with feathers. Tom saw that Spiros was circling them — but with no real body, there was nothing the ghost phoenix could do to help.

The girl stabbed at Tom, and he locked the blade of her sword with his hilt, grabbed her arm, and pulled her toward him. He held his own blade at her throat, leaning far out over Epos's body.

"You've lost," said Tom. "You can't defeat me."

She struggled, but he gripped her sword arm even more tightly.

"Tell me who you are," he said in her car.

The girl stopped struggling and smiled cruelly. "My name is Sethrina," she hissed. "Surely I remind you of someone."

Now it was clear to Tom. "You work for Malvel!" he said.

"One day, everyone will work for Malvel," the girl replied.

"Never!" shouted Tom. "While there's blood in my veins, I'll keep Avantia free. Run back to your master and tell him I said that."

Tom released Sethrina's arm; he had to go after Elenna. But immediately, Sethrina lunged with her sword. Tom blocked her strike easily.

"Don't you know when to give up?" he shouted. "You can't win, and if you're not careful, it's *your* phoenix that will get killed."

Sethrina smiled wickedly. "Oh, Tom, you don't want to kill my phoenix, believe me. That would be very bad for your precious Avantia. . . ."

There was a screech and Tom looked up to see Spiros hovering in the air above. Suddenly, he saw that Spiros and the black phoenix were exactly the same size, with identical beaks and talons. Beneath the black phoenix's layer of grime, Tom could just make out the same red scales as . . . Then the awful realization hit him: The black phoenix had Spiros's body!

Sethrina was watching his face closely. "Ah,

you've understood!" She patted the phoenix's neck. "Meet Nawdren."

"That body belongs to Spiros!" shouted Tom.

"Ha!" laughed Sethrina. "Nawdren has nothing to do with Spiros. Or, at least, she never will again!"

Then she lunged at Tom with her sword.

He dodged the blow and aimed his own sword at Nawdren's beak. If he could distract the evil phoenix, it would at least give him time to help Elenna. He hit the beak with the flat of his sword, as hard as he could. The phoenix drew her head back and screeched in agony, wheeling away through the clouds. Tom heard Sethrina's cry of anger as she was carried away.

Immediately, he steered Epos in a steep dive down through the clouds.

"I'm coming, Elenna!" he called out, but dread

filled his heart. What was waiting for him on the icy plains of Avantia? Would he find his friend in time to help her? If he lost Elenna,would he ever be able to complete this Beast Quest alone?

To be continued . . .

Story Two

Chapter One

The Land of Ice

THE LAND OF THE ICY PLAINS WAS WHITE WITH patches of blue where the ice was thin. The bitter wind had carved icebergs into strange shapes. Spiros flew beside Tom and Epos.

"We have to find Elenna!" Tom shouted.

The flame bird headed down to the ice shelf, her massive shadow rippling over the land below.

Suddenly, Spiros squawked and dropped away. Tom could see where she was heading — a patch of brown lying in the middle of a frozen lake. Elenna! As he guided Epos to follow, he saw his shield on the ice a few paces away from her.

Epos landed on the frozen surface, her talons sending up shards of ice. Spiros floated to the ground without a sound. Tom leaped off the flame bird's back and rushed to his friend. The ice creaked beneath his feet. Beside Elenna's body was a hole in the ice, and Tom could see the water below, lapping at the edges. He knelt down next to Elenna. Her clothes were soaking wet. He didn't understand: Had she fallen through the ice and then pulled herself out of the freezing water? Surely that was impossible. Her lips were turning blue. Ice crystals, like tiny jewels, had already begun to form on her eyelashes.

"Elenna!" he whispered, then put his head on her soaking chest and listened. She still had a heartbeat. Placing his hand by her open mouth, he felt the slight warmth of shallow, regular breathing.

She was alive!

"Elenna, it's me, Tom," he said, shaking her shoulder a little.

Her eyelids fluttered, then she opened her eyes. "Tom?"

"Can you get up?" he asked.

Elenna sat up carefully, then let out a deep shiver. "I . . . I'm so cold," she stammered.

Tom knew that if Elenna didn't get warm soon, she would die. He lifted her onto his back and carried her to the edge of the frozen lake. In the shelter of a tall ice stack, they sat down in the snow. Epos hopped over to them, extending a wing, which burst into low, gentle flames, bathing Elenna in heat. Not for the first time, Tom was thankful to have the good Beasts of Avantia on his side.

When Elenna had stopped shaking, Tom asked, "What happened? Did you catch my shield?"

"Yes," said Elenna. "As I fell, I thought I was

dead for sure. But then the shield came hurtling toward me and I heard your voice. As soon as I caught it, the magic of Cypher's tear helped me to slow down."

"But the hole in the ice?" Tom asked.

"Well, I was so close to the ground, and traveling so fast, the shield couldn't save me completely. I remember seeing the lake coming toward me. I shut my eyes. That's the last thing I remember. I must have smashed right through the ice."

"But how could you have come up again?" said Tom in bewilderment.

"I don't know. . . ." said Elenna.

Then a huge roar burst from behind the ice stack, dislodging a layer of snow, which fell in a fine powder around their heads. There was a series of crunching sounds, as though something large was padding toward them, and Spiros let out a soft call. Tartok stood proudly before them.

"She must have plucked me out of the water," said Elenna. "She saved my life! Thank you, Tartok."

The giant snow monster of the icy plains bellowed, ruffling their hair with the force of her roar. Then she turned and strode away into the snow. As she disappeared, a sudden flash in the sky made them look up. Spiros hovered above them, beating her golden wings.

"We have to get going," said Tom. "If we wait here for too long, Sethrina will find us."

"Sethrina?" asked Elenna.

Tom explained what he had learned about Seth's sister and Nawdren.

"So Nawdren is Spiros's body, separated from Spiros's spirit to carry out Malvel's evil!" Elenna exclaimed, getting to her feet. But as she did so, she winced and let out a small cry. "My ankle!" Tom looked down at Elenna's ankle. It was red and swollen. "I think it's broken! My body was so cold I didn't even realize until just now!" she said in despair, sitting back down in the snow.

"Don't worry," said Tom. "Epos's talon can help." He slid back across the ice and retrieved his shield. At Elenna's side, he detached the feather. Its magical healing powers had already helped him on previous Quests. Tom held it to her ankle. It warmed in his hand.

"It's working!" said Elenna.

Tom stared at the ankle. Slowly, the swelling disappeared, and the redness faded to Elenna's normal skin color.

"Try standing on it," Tom suggested.

Elenna pushed herself to her feet and gingerly put her weight onto the injured leg. A smile broke across her face. "It's much better!" she cried out.

They scrambled onto Epos's back, and the flame bird shook the loose snow from her talons. Spiros flapped her wings, rising high above them.

"It looks as if she's ready to go, too!" said Elenna.

"We'll have to be careful," said Tom as Epos took to the sky. "I have a feeling that we haven't seen the last of Sethrina."

But as they followed Spiros, Tom felt ready for anything Malvel could throw at him. It was time to rescue Uncle Henry and Aunt Maria!

Chapter Two

The Underworld

Gusts battered Tom and Elenna as they clung to Epos's feathers, and Tom had to brush the snow and ice crystals from his face to see properly. Spiros was flying through the sky at amazing speed, and Epos was working hard to keep up. Snowflakes sizzled as they met the flames along her wings.

"I don't know how Spiros can find her way in these conditions," said Elenna.

"It's the magic of her All-Sight that's guiding her," said Tom.

Spiros squawked urgently and turned in the air, her wings glowing.

"She's trying to tell us something," said Elenna.

The ghost phoenix suddenly twisted her glittering wings and began to descend. Epos cut through the wind in pursuit.

"This is it!" shouted Tom, as the air streamed around him. "She's found my aunt and uncle!"

They flew down more steeply, picking up speed all the time. Tom could feel the force rippling his cheeks. Through an eddying swirl of snow, Tom saw the ice fields below. They were heading straight for them. He felt Elenna tense as she held on to him.

Epos drew in her wings. Her body was almost vertical as it shot to earth.

"Tom, we're going to crash!" shouted Elenna.

"We have to trust Spiros," said Tom, gritting his teeth.

She didn't pull up. It looked as though her ghostly outline would smash to pieces against the ice, but she slid through the frozen layer without a sound.

Tom fought the urge to pull with all his might on Epos's feathers. "I've put my faith in Spiros till now," he shouted. "While there's blood in my veins, we'll follow her to the end."

The snowy ground rushed toward them. Epos stretched out her talons. A spark appeared between them, then grew into a ball of flame, burning almost white with heat.

Epos hurled the fireball at the spot where Spiros had disappeared. It smashed into the frozen wasteland, showering sparks. Then the ice was gone, replaced by a crater. In the middle of the hole, the fireball sank into a patch of boiling sea. Epos and her passengers dived into the chasm.

We'll drown! Tom thought. But the fireball bored a tunnel straight down through the water. Elenna cried out in surprise and Tom gasped. Epos plunged after her fireball as the sea closed in behind them. Tom and Elenna were in a tunnel of air created by Epos, deep below the ocean.

They quickly reached the seafloor. Limp weeds lay flat on the sand, and a crab scuttled for shelter beneath a rock covered in bright yellow tendrils. The fireball had spread out around them like a dome, holding back the weight of water. Tom felt the spray dry on his face as the flames warmed him. It was as though they were in another world. Elenna was staring around, her mouth open in wonder.

"This is powerful magic!" said Tom.

"Who would have thought?" Elenna said, stroking Epos's feathers. "A bird at the bottom of the sea!"

The light dimmed, and the dome of flame above their heads inched closer. Epos let out a warning squawk.

"Hurry, Tom," said Elenna. "The magic is fading!"

Tom climbed off Epos's back, and the flame bird hopped aside, revealing something on the seafloor. Tom bent to inspect it.

"Look, Elenna!" he said. "It's a trapdoor!"

"Where can it lead?" asked Elenna.

The walls of seawater were closing in again, and the fireball burned less fiercely around them.

"There's only one way to find out," said Tom.

He seized the chain and yanked on it. The trapdoor didn't move.

"Try again," said Elenna. "You can do it."

Tom thought of his golden breastplate. Its magic gave him extra strength. Still, it might not be enough.

He looped the chain around his waist and clenched his fists under one of the links. He took a huge breath, dug his heels into the wet sand, and pushed with every muscle in his legs. The trapdoor moved a finger's width. Tom didn't stop. His kneecaps felt as if they were about to burst apart, and his heart was racing, but still he pulled. Finally, the trapdoor lifted open.

"Quick! Jump in," Tom shouted at Elenna and Epos. The good Beast plunged into the tunnel. The seawater was splashing Tom's hair now. Taking the strain on his arms, he pulled himself along the rope toward the open crack. The protective fire around him was almost out. When he was close to the open trapdoor, he let the coiled chain fall around his feet and jumped down. The door crashed shut behind him and he heard the rush of water behind the door. They'd made it!

Tom realized he was lying on cold, wet rock. It was pitch-black. He couldn't even see his hand in front of his face.

"Tom?" Elenna's voice echoed around them.

"I'm here!" he said, picking himself up and stumbling through the darkness. His hand closed around Elenna's wrist.

"What now?" she asked.

"We need light," said Tom.

The shape of two wings appeared ahead of them, doused in flame. Epos! As the fire grew, their surroundings became clear. Tom stared about him in astonishment.

"What is this place?" gasped Elenna.

"It must be an underworld!" Tom replied.

CHAPTER THREE

THE CAVERNS OF DANGER

THEY WERE STANDING IN A SMALL RECESS AT the edge of a massive cavern. Huge stalactites descended from the cave roof, and great pillars of rock grew from the floor, where pools of sticky brown slime boiled and belched out yellow smoke. A rotting smell hung in the air.

Elenna held her hand to her nose. "This place stinks!" she said.

The light from Epos's wings cast sinister shadows across the cave roof. Anything could be lurking in wait for them. At the edge of the cavern, a number of tunnels led in different directions. The entrances were like black mouths in the cave walls. It was totally silent, other than the regular dripping of water and bubbling of the slime pools.

"This must be some sort of mine," said Elenna. "Those tunnels are man-made."

Spiros was floating in the air beside a tunnel at the far side of the underground grotto.

"She wants us to follow her," said Tom.

"I'm not sure about this," said Elenna. "How do we know which path to take?"

"We have to trust Spiros's All-Sight," Tom replied. "She wouldn't take us into danger."

Tom led the way across the cavern, hopping from rock to rock between the pools. Elenna and Epos followed, the winged flame cawing softly. They reached the spot where Spiros was waiting for them. Tom stared into the blackness of the tunnel entrance. Even he felt a tingle of doubt.

"Let me check the compass," he said, pulling it from his pocket and holding it up. Elenna came to look over his shoulder. The needle of the compass pointed to Destiny.

"It's settled, then," said Tom. "This is the way to go."

The ghost phoenix turned and drifted into the tunnel. Tom drew his sword and followed close behind with Elenna. Behind them came Epos, lighting the way with her flaming feathers.

The tunnel twisted and turned, and Tom could tell there was a slight downward slope to the cave floor. They were heading deeper underground, farther away from the land he knew. But the Beasts showed no fear, and Tom forced his own heartbeat to slow.

Elenna put her hand on his arm. "Tom," she hissed. "There's a light!"

Spiros turned and cawed softly to urge them on.

Elenna was right. As well as the glow from Epos's feathers, there was another source of light in front of them. They pressed on, and soon Tom saw a torch hanging on the tunnel wall. The lights sent flickering shadows across the passage.

Suddenly, there was a noise from up ahead — a high-pitched squeaking and the sound of something scraping along rock. Tom froze. It was like the scratching of claws.

"What is it?" asked Elenna.

Before Tom could answer, a rat scurried along the tunnel floor. He breathed a sigh of relief. "If that's the worst we have to deal with, I'll be happy."

There were more rats the farther they went, and the stench in the air grew worse. The Beasts didn't seem to notice, but for Tom it was overwhelming. He tried not to breathe through his nose, but even then he could taste the tang of rotting flesh.

“Was that a voice?” Elenna said.

Tom cupped a hand to his ear. A faint cry sounded through the stillness. “It’s my aunt Maria!” he said. “Come on!”

⟶ Chapter Four ⟵

Rescue!

Tom charged along the tunnel, past Spiros. He could hear Elenna's footsteps close behind him. All the time, the voices ahead were getting louder. He ignored the foul stench in the air and the rats that scurried out of his way.

Rounding a corner, he reached a huge wooden door. Massive bronze hinges attached it to the bare rock of the tunnel. He tried to push it open, but it was locked from the inside.

"Help us!" came a voice.

It was Uncle Henry!

Tom threw himself at the door, but the lock held.

"Can't you use your magic strength?" said Elenna.

Tom rammed the door again with his shoulder. Nothing happened.

"It must be enchanted with Malvel's magic!" he said. "Stand back."

Tom put down his shield and gripped the hilt of his sword in both hands, lifting it over his head. Then, with all the power he could muster, he brought the blade down on the middle of the door.

The wood split open and one of the hinges broke away. The sound of the impact echoed through the tunnel. Epos screeched with surprise.

Beyond the smashed doorway loomed an enormous chamber. The walls rose up in sheer slopes. Dangling high above the stony ground, with coils of rope wrapped around their middles, were Uncle Henry and Aunt Maria. The thick rope stretched high into the cavern above, attached somewhere out of sight. Tom's aunt and uncle squirmed when they saw him, setting the ropes creaking.

"Tom! Thank goodness!" said Aunt Maria. "Help us down!"

Tom quickly scanned the walls of the cavern, but they were completely sheer, and slick with water and moss. There wasn't a handhold in sight.

"Don't panic!" he said. "I'll think of something."

Perhaps Epos could burn through the ropes. . . . No, that was a foolish idea. His aunt and uncle would plunge to their deaths. What they needed was something to land on. Something soft . . . like phoenix feathers . . .

"Epos!" said Tom. But the flame bird seemed to read his mind — she was already taking to the air, lighting the upper reaches of the cavern. She let out an echoing squawk as she swooped down beneath his aunt and uncle and hovered there, so their feet brushed against her feathers.

"She's supporting them," said Elenna. "Can you use your sword to cut the ropes?"

"How?" said Tom. "I can't fly up there!"

"Throw it," said Elenna.

"What if I miss?" he said. "I might injure someone."

"We trust you," shouted Uncle Henry. "We know you won't let us down."

His uncle's words fired Tom with courage. He took careful aim, then hurled his sword through the air. It spun in dizzying arcs across the cavern, the blade whistling, and sliced smoothly through both ropes. Tom's aunt and uncle tumbled safely into Epos's cushioned feathers. The sword clattered onto the cavern floor.

"Well done!" shouted Elenna.

Tom rushed over to where the flame bird had landed. "I'm so happy I found you," he said, hugging his aunt and uncle tightly. "I thought I might never —"

"Shush, nephew," said Uncle Henry. "We knew you'd come. Malvel can't stand in the way of courage like yours." He turned to Elenna. "And Tom's lucky to have a companion like you."

"Thank you," Elenna said. She gave a mischievous smile. "I'm just the brains of the team!"

"She's not bad with a bow and arrow, either," said Tom, laughing. Elenna blushed. "And we wouldn't even be here without Epos."

Uncle Henry stared at the Beast. "I . . . I've never seen a . . ."

"She's the winged flame," said Tom. "A good Beast. There's nothing to fear."

Epos ruffled her feathers and cawed.

"Incredible," said Tom's uncle. "Well, my thanks to all of you."

Tom's heart felt light with joy. His aunt and uncle were free, and Malvel was overcome. . . .

Then the sound of slow clapping emerged from the gloom on the other side of the chamber.

Tom turned. "Who's there?" he said.

"Well done!" said Sethrina, stepping into the light of the chamber. Beside her lumbered Nawdren, beak drooling thick saliva, and black talons scraping the cave floor. Epos rose to her feet and screeched in alarm.

Tom's hand darted to his hip, but his scabbard was empty.

Sethrina bent down and picked up something from the ground. “Looking for this?” she sneered, holding up Tom’s sword.

“Give that back!” said Tom. “Let’s make this a fair fight.”

Sethrina’s laughter filled the echoing space. “What makes you think I want a fair fight? My brother told me how stupid you are. Poor, brave, stupid Tom. Didn’t you realize this was a trap?”

“Oh no!” said Aunt Maria.

“Drop the sword!” shouted Elenna. Tom turned to see that she’d strung her bow and was pointing an arrow at Sethrina. Nawdren gave an angry roar, filling the air with a heavy green mist. Tom moved to shield his aunt and uncle.

Elenna fired the arrow. It sped toward Sethrina, but with a deft flick of her wrist, she chopped the shaft in half.

"It'll take more than your pins to stop me," she mocked. "I've got Malvel's magic on my side."

Tom felt for the fragment of horseshoe on his shield. Ever since he'd freed Tagus, it gave him the ability to move at super speed. He'd need that now.

"I've got some tricks of my own," he said. He shot forward, and before Sethrina could draw breath, he slammed into her. Tom's sword fell from her hands.

Sethrina drew her sword and leaped toward him, swinging her blade. Tom rolled beneath the attack and plucked his sword from the ground. He turned to face her.

"Now the odds are even," he said. "Let's find out how good you really are."

Chapter Five

The Final Fight

Sethrina lowered her weapon and arched one black eyebrow.

"Don't you dare to fight me?" asked Tom.

Sethrina smiled and sheathed her sword. "Why should I duel with you?" she said. "I have a Beast for that. Nawdren!"

At her command, the black phoenix stepped forward. Spiros, who had been resting near the door of the cavern, let out a cry of despair. Epos screeched and moved toward Tom. He held up his hand to tell the winged flame to stop, then raised his sword. This was his battle.

Nawdren spread her wings, which spanned half the cavern, and leaped in the air, her talons outstretched. Tom pushed his aunt and uncle aside, and Nawdren slammed into the ground a shield's width from where they had been standing. The Beast smashed Tom off his feet with one of her wings, sending him flying to the edge of the cave.

Tom climbed dizzily to his feet. To his horror he saw Nawdren rearing to her full height above his aunt and uncle. Her black beak looked as sharp as an ax.

"No!" he shouted.

Suddenly, in a flash of red, Epos descended onto Nawdren's back. High-pitched screeches pierced the cavern, and black and red feathers fluttered in the air.

"Uncle Henry," Tom yelled, "you have to get out of here!"

Nawdren threw Epos off her back, and the flame bird landed in a heavy heap by the cave wall. Then the black phoenix turned to attack Tom's uncle again. Tom swung his sword at the evil Beast. The blade rebounded off Nawdren's beak with a sound like a blacksmith's hammer, and sent Nawdren reeling backward.

Tom's uncle and aunt darted toward the broken doorway.

"They're getting away!" shouted Sethrina.

Nawdren turned her massive head and bounded across the cavern after them. Tom threw a desperate glance at Epos. She was moving, but only a little. There was nothing Tom could do.

Suddenly, an arrow buried itself in Nawdren's chest feathers. Elenna! The Beast staggered. Tom's friend unleashed another shaft, which thudded in next to the first. "Get back, slave of Malvel!" Elenna cried.

Nawdren's howl of pain filled the dank air. Uncle Henry and Aunt Maria slipped through the doorway. The evil Beast bent her head to her chest and snapped the arrows away, flinging them to the cavern floor. Her eyes glowed silver with anger. Elenna fired another arrow, but Nawdren batted it away with her wing. Then she charged at Elenna.

Tom dashed to help. He swung his sword and felt it slice into Nawdren's wing. The Beast screeched again and rose off the ground. She hovered, flapping one wing frantically, the injured one half-folded into her side.

Spiros was suddenly beside her, darting at the wound.

"What's she doing?" asked Elenna. "She can't help — she's only a ghost!"

Spiros wheeled away, then dived again, letting out a desperate wail. Epos sent a cry from the cavern floor.

"She's trying to attack the wound," said Tom.

"Finish the boy!" shouted Sethrina. "Malvel wants him dead."

Nawdren twisted away from Spiros and swooped down, her talons whistling through the air. Tom lifted his shield and felt the weight of the bird crash into the wood. He was knocked to the ground as the black phoenix retreated for another attack.

"Your shield!" cried Elenna.

Tom clambered up and looked at his shield. It was gouged where a talon had torn into the wood. This Beast was more powerful than any he had faced before.

"Your magic is no match for Malvel's!" Sethrina laughed.

Tom gripped his shield tighter, and called upon the power of his golden chain mail. His chest swelled with courage. But he knew he couldn't defeat Nawdren here on the cave floor. He needed a plan. *I have to get into the air*, he thought.

The evil phoenix dived again. Tom ducked under her stabbing beak, then rolled between her talons, his nostrils filling with the stink of rotting feathers. There, in front of him, was Epos. Tom sprinted toward the flame bird and leaped onto her back. She immediately extended her flaming wings and flew up.

Nawdren soared after them as Tom was carried to the upper reaches of the cavern. He clutched the feathers tightly as Epos twisted to avoid Nawdren's talons.

I must get above her! he thought. Epos seemed to understand and flapped her wings harder to rise above the evil Beast. Tom saw his chance — and leaped off Epos's back. For a moment, he was weightless, then he crashed onto Nawdren's wing. His fingers struggled to grip the slimy feathers. He stabbed with his sword and pierced the wing again. Nawdren convulsed and Tom was thrown through the air. The cave floor rushed toward him, but the magic giant's tear in his shield slowed his fall. He hit the ground hard, jolting his knees.

Nawdren squawked and drops of black blood splashed on the cavern floor. Sethrina's laugh pierced the cave.

"If you kill her," she said, "Spiros will never have her body back!"

As Nawdren hovered, Spiros bravely flew at her again, darting toward the injured wing. Nawdren twisted in the air, not letting her ghost draw near. Finally, Tom understood.

"Elenna," Tom shouted. "Spiros is trying to

reclaim her body. She's trying to get in through the wounds."

"No!" said Sethrina. "You're wrong!"

But Tom could hear panic in Sethrina's voice. "Ignore her!" he said. "We have to keep attacking. It's the only way!"

Chapter Six

The Return of Spiros

Elenna unleashed an arrow toward Nawdren. It fell short — the Beast was too high.

Sethrina burst out laughing. "You've only got three arrows left!" she cried.

"Elenna, use Epos!" said Tom.

His friend dashed toward the flame bird. A frown creased Sethrina's pale forehead. She dived toward Elenna, swinging her sword. Tom hurled his shield, and it spun through the air to catch Sethrina on the temple. She sprawled on the ground, out cold.

Now Nawdren was only the evil Beast they faced. Elenna climbed onto Epos's back.

"You need to distract Nawdren!" said Tom.

"But how will you get up there?" asked Elenna.

"Leave that to me," he replied. "Wait for my signal."

Epos sprang into the air, lighting the gloom with her wings. Nawdren swooped down to attack, and Tom's heart almost stopped. It looked as though Epos would be torn to pieces by the black phoenix's talons. But at the very last moment, the flame bird dodged to the side and rose above Nawdren. The evil Beast looped up to attack a second time.

"Now!" shouted Tom.

Elenna bravely let go of Epos's feathers and placed the first of her last three arrows to the bow's string. One after the other, she fired all three at the approaching phoenix. They whistled through the air and thudded into the Beast's feathers. Nawdren let out a loud screech.

Tom took a deep breath. *This is my only chance*, he thought.

Using his magical speed, he ran at the cavern wall, then leaped into the air. He took one, two, three, four massive strides, climbing the rock, then pushed himself off. At the same moment, he twisted in the air and threw out his arms. He had no shield to stop him from falling now. His hands closed around the frayed end of the dangling rope in the center of the cavern.

With his heart pounding, he scrambled up the rope, hand over hand, until his arms burned. Nawdren was still keening in pain as Tom climbed below her. He tugged his sword from its sheath and lunged at the black phoenix. The blade cut a long gash at the base of her wing. Her cries pierced

the air as hot ash and black blood sprayed across the cave.

Tom couldn't hold on any longer and let go of the rope, tumbling downward.

But instead of landing on hard rock, Tom bounced into something soft and warm. He opened his eyes to see Epos's feathers. Elenna sat astride her neck. The good Beast must have swooped down to save him.

"Thanks!" said Tom breathlessly.

He and Elenna jumped off as Epos landed. Above, Nawdren was frantically flapping her one good wing in a desperate attempt to stay aloft. The other hung limply, only half-attached to her body. Despite the battle, Tom almost felt sorry for the Beast.

"Look," whispered Elenna. "Spiros!"

The ghost phoenix swept through the cave toward the injured Beast. The green light from her eyes faded and her diamond talons dimmed to gray. As she approached Nawdren, her body seemed to become more transparent, like a wisp of cloud stretched in the wind. The cloud wrapped itself around Nawdren's body and Spiros was gone. Suddenly, the ash stopped falling.

The white cloud poured into the wound on the evil phoenix's wing. Nawdren's cries became weaker and she sank through the air. Tom watched as she came to rest on the cavern floor. Her black, slimy body was completely still.

"Oh no!" said Elenna. "What have we done?"

Tom rushed forward. He sank to his knees beside the huge body of the dead bird.

A soft cawing made him look up. The black feathers on the motionless head were glowing, first brown, then red. The color spread across the feathers on the phoenix's back and then along the wings. Soon they were as bright as rubies, and

Tom had to shield his eyes and step back. Elenna stood beside him, her mouth open. The Beast lifted its head and leaped up on its jeweled talons. Finally, the eyes opened, shedding emerald light across the cavern. Nawdren had been transformed!

With a whoosh, the phoenix shot out her wings. Her injuries had magically healed. She lifted herself into the air above them, scattering dappled light into the darkness.

"It's Spiros!" said Elenna, with tears of joy in her eyes.

Epos cawed with delight and spiraled upward into the cavern, adding her own light to that of her fellow phoenix.

Tom caught sight of his aunt and uncle at the doorway of the chamber, gazing up. "It's safe!" he called to them.

They walked hesitantly into the room, hand in hand, transfixed by the incredible new Beast. The magnificent phoenix swept over to Tom and Elenna, and lowered her head. Tom stroked her beautiful golden beak, and she cawed softly.

"Nawdren?" said a weak voice. Tom spun around to see Sethrina sitting up and rubbing her head.

"Nawdren's gone," he said coldly.

"And Spiros has her body back!" added Elenna.

Horror contorted Sethrina's features. "It can't be!" she said. "Malvel's magic is too powerful." She reached for her sword, but Tom was too quick. He knocked it from her hand, and stood with the point of his blade at her neck.

"Good magic always overpowers evil," he said.

"This time, perhaps," spat Sethrina. "But I'm not afraid to die."

Tom looked into her dark eyes. Her hatred shone out. "I don't want to kill people," he said. "That's what makes us different."

Sethrina's mouth twisted in anger. "That's what makes you weak," she said.

"How can we get out?" said Elenna, ignoring the other girl's taunts and turning to Tom. "I'd rather not swim through the icy water."

"She must know," said Tom's aunt, pointing at Sethrina. "She brought us here."

Sethrina lifted her chin in defiance. "Why should I tell you?" she sneered. "You'll have me locked in King Hugo's dungeon by nightfall."

Tom looked at Elenna, raising his eyebrows. They needed Sethrina, and she knew it.

Elenna nodded. "Tell us how to get out of this place, and you can go free."

"Just like that?" said Sethrina, her voice tinged with suspicion.

"Yes," said Tom, "but you must promise never to return to Avantia again."

Sethrina frowned, then sank back, defeated. "Very well," she said.

Elenna gathered her arrows from the cavern floor and put one of them back in her bow, aiming its sharp point at Sethrina.

"Show us the way out," she said.

⤚ Chapter Seven ⤙

Farewell to the Phoenix

Sethrina climbed to her feet and walked to the far side of the cavern. Tom, Elenna, Uncle Henry, and Aunt Maria followed. Spiros and Epos hopped behind. It looked as though they were all heading toward a solid wall, but Sethrina stopped in front of it.

"Where now?" asked Tom.

Sethrina placed her hand on the slick rock and pushed. "Is no one going to help me?" she asked.

Tom came forward and leaned his shoulder into the wall. It wasn't rock, he realized — just wood disguised to look like rock. He pushed again. A low grating sound echoed in the vast space, before a crack as tall as four men appeared in the cavern wall, casting a shaft of light into the dim cave. *A secret door!* With the help of his magical strength, the door swung open. A blast of stale air filled his nostrils.

Beyond was a tunnel, roughly hewn into the bare rock. The passage was tall and narrow, but Spiros tucked her wings into her side and squeezed through.

They reached the bottom of a spiral staircase cut into the rock. Tom looked up. Above, through the heart of the coiling steps, he could see a pale circle of greenish light.

"We're almost there," he said.

"Perhaps it's a trap," said Elenna.

Tom's aunt and uncle shared a look of uncertainty.

“I’ll go first,” said Tom. “Epos and Spiros can fly up the middle. They’ll alert us to any dangers.”

As soon as they were all on the steps, the two birds took to the air and soared past them. Moments later, their caws of joy drifted back down.

“It’s safe,” Tom said.

Suddenly, he felt a shove in the back and he tripped on the steps. Sethrina darted past him and up the steps. When she stood on the final curve of the staircase, she looked back with a grin.

“Farewell, fools!” she shouted. “We’ll meet again!”

Elenna started to set off after her, but Tom held her back.

“Leave her,” he said. “We promised her freedom, anyway.”

Sethrina raced up the last few steps and was gone.

At the top of the staircase, a green glow filled the tunnel, and soon Tom could see why. Chinks of daylight shone through a curtain of leaves. Tom pushed them aside and stepped out among trees. He found himself standing on a ledge beneath an outcrop of rock. Below, a river flowed like a silver ribbon through a lush green valley. Far off, the blue sea twinkled in the sunlight. He could see Sethrina, a distant speck, running down the mountainside toward the valley.

"We must be in the northern mountains," said Tom. "We're safe again." He felt a hand on his shoulder and turned to see Uncle Henry looking down at him with pride in his eyes.

"What you did was very brave," he said.

Tom's aunt nodded in agreement. "Without you, we would have died," she said.

"It's time for you to go home to Errinel," Tom responded.

"How?" asked Aunt Maria. "It must be several days' walk from here. We're not as young as we used to be, you know!"

Tom laughed. "Epos will give you a ride."

The great Beast squawked as though she understood.

Uncle Henry climbed onto Epos's back, then helped Aunt Maria to scramble up. "What about you and your friend? Aren't you coming with us?" he asked.

Tom looked at Elenna and Spiros. "No. While Malvel is still free to wreak havoc, our job isn't done. We have to go back to Storm and Silver. There'll be more Beast Quests to come."

Tom's uncle nodded in understanding. "Be careful, both of you. And good luck!"

Epos took a few steps to the edge of the ledge. She opened her massive wings and leaped off, soaring over the valley below. Tom watched the majestic Beast disappear into the distance. Uncle Henry and Aunt Maria would be back in Errinel by nightfall.

Tom turned to Spiros. "Time for you to go home, too," he said, patting the phoenix's wing.

Spiros dipped her golden beak in a bow of thanks, then ruffled her ruby feathers. She unfolded her wings, which gleamed in the sun and cast a shadow over Tom's head. He held his breath. Then the phoenix sprang into the air, giving out a huge squawk that carried across the empty sky.

"Oh, Tom, she's amazing!" gasped Elenna.

"And now she's back where she belongs," said Tom. "Guarding the skies of Avantia. We've rescued my aunt and uncle — but we've helped

Spiros, too. This has turned out to be a bigger Quest than I'd ever imagined."

Spiros swooped past them a final time, then glided toward the horizon.

"Tom! Look!" cried Elenna, twisting around.

Tom turned and gasped in surprise. There, silhouetted on the slope above them, were four huge shapes: Ferno the Fire Dragon, his mouth glowing with flame; Cypher the Mountain Giant grinning broadly and revealing his brown teeth; Tagus the Night Horse, stamping the ground with his enormous hooves; and Tartok the Ice Beast, hammering her white-furred chest with her palms. Tom glanced back toward the sea and saw a flash of rainbow colors as Sepron the Sea Serpent broke the waves. He felt his shield vibrate on his arm. His friends had gathered to congratulate him on the completion of his latest Quest.

"These are the best friends I could have," he said, laughing and waving at the Beasts. "After you, Elenna!"

"You'll never be alone on your Quests," said Elenna.

Tom stared out across Avantia, his home. It was safe again — for now.

"Let's go and find Storm and Silver," he said, setting off down a slope. There would be more difficult Quests to come, but whatever lay ahead of him, Tom knew he would do his best — for his friends and for Avantia.

Don't miss Tom's

first quest . . .

Ferno

The Fire Dragon

Read the first

chapter now!

Chapter One

The Mysterious Fire

Tom stared hard at his enemy. "Surrender, villain!" he cried, waving his sword above his head. "Surrender, or taste my blade!"

The sword was only a poker, and his enemy was a sack of hay hanging from a tree in the heart of the wood. But then, Tom was not a knight. He was training to be a blacksmith. The closest he came to thrilling quests was when he ran errands for his uncle Henry, who worked the village forge.

Today, Tom was taking a sack of newly mended tools to Farmer Gretlin. Along the way, he had stopped in the forest to practice his sword-fighting moves on the dummy he had made a few weeks ago. He trained whenever he could. If he ever had the chance to have a real sword fight, he'd be ready!

Tom gave the target a firm blow with the poker. "One day I'll be the finest swordsman in all of the kingdom of Avantia," he announced. "Even better than my father, Taladon the Swift!"

Tom had heard many people in the village praise Taladon's swordsmanship. But he had never seen it for himself. Tom's mother had died of a fever when he was just a baby. That same day, his father had left on a mysterious quest and never returned. As Head of Errinel village and Tom's closest relative, Uncle Henry had announced that he and his wife, Maria, would raise him as their own son.

Tom was grateful to his uncle and trained hard as a blacksmith's apprentice. But he often dreamed of leaving Errinel, just as his father had. He wanted to taste adventure for real — dreams just weren't enough anymore. But most of all, he wanted to find his father and ask him why he had left.

Tom shoved the poker back into the sack of tools. "One day I'll know the truth," he swore.

Summer was giving way to autumn, and Tom shivered as he walked beneath the shadows cast by the trees' heavy branches. It was hard going along the overgrown forest path. Branches tore at Tom's clothes and scratched his face. Stumbling over tree roots, Tom struggled on. As he neared the edge of the woods, he smelled something strange.

Smoke! he thought as the sharp smell caught at the back of his throat.

He stopped and looked around. Through the trees to his left he could hear a faint crackling as a wave of warm air hit him.

Fire!

Tom began to push his way through the trees. Heart pounding, he forced his way through a thicket and burst into the field. The golden wheat had been burned to black stubble. A thin veil of smoke hung in the air, small flames still licked at the edges of the field. Tom stared in horror. What had happened?

A shadow fell over him. Tom looked up and blinked. For a second he thought he saw a dark, fleeting shape disappear behind a hill in the distance. Had his eyes been playing tricks on him?

"Who's there?"

Through the smoke, Tom saw a man stamping across the field. Forgetting the shadow, he hurried forward to meet him.

"Did you come through the woods?" Gretlin demanded. "Did you see anyone who could have done this?"

Tom shook his head. "No one! I didn't see a soul in the woods."

"There's evil at work here," said Gretlin, his eyes flashing angrily. "Only ten minutes ago, this wheat was as tall as your shoulders. I was working in the barn when I heard a strange noise, like a fierce wind. I rushed outside to find . . . *this.*" Gretlin stared at the blackened field. "Mark my words — no ordinary fire did this. Just like no ordinary fire took John Blake's horses."

A shiver of fear went through Tom. John Blake lived at the edge of Errinel, and two weeks ago he had lost three of his horses during the night. Their bones were found the next day, in a smoking pit at the foot of the valley — roasted and picked clean. "The old ones are talking in the village," said Gretlin, shaking his head. "They say dark forces are gathering. . . ."

Tom looked around at the burned field and felt

a wave of anger. Someone needed to stop this. If only he was older! *I'd do it*, he thought. *I'd stop things like this happening in our kingdom.*

"Go back to the forge, Tom," Gretlin said. "Tell your uncle what's happened here! I'm worried that Errinel is cursed — and maybe all of us along with it!"